BLESSED ASSURANCE

BY

KATRINA OKALSKI

BLESSED ASSURANCE
ISBN-13: 978-1-105-19197-8

Cover Image: © http://aspringstead.deviantart.com/
Cover Design: Anne Springstead

For bulk order prices or any other inquiries, please contact www.lulu.com

CHAPTER ONE

The procession of priests moved slowly up the center aisle of the dimly lit church, heads bowed and hands clasped in solemn silence. Mackenzie stood silently among the throngs of people, religious and otherwise, who came to pay their respects to this beloved and gentle man. She took a moment to look around the church that she loved and where she spent such a large portion of her childhood. The building itself was beginning to show its age. The plaster walls were cracking and were desperately in need of some paint. The lead in the stained glass windows was likewise beginning to peel, distorting the artwork that they held within. Some things hadn't changed, however. The smells, for one, were the same. Mackenzie breathed deep the smell of incense and flowers, smiling to herself at the memories they conjured up. The sound of the organ remained the same as well. Not only was it the same one hundred-year-old pipe organ that she remembered singing along to as a child, but the woman playing the organ was also the same. Ella Cummings spent fifty glorious years behind that organ and she showed no signs of slowing down.

Gingerly touching the wood of the pew in front of her, Mackenzie was flooded with memories of a troubled time in her life. A time not soon forgotten. She bowed her head, her reddish-brown hair falling forward and framing her face, hiding the tears that were beginning to fall. She was all grown up now, along with her two siblings, all with families of their own, but they all agreed that Fr. Anthony was the best thing that ever happened to them.

Mackenzie sat down in the pew, following the lead of the other mourners. Closing her eyes, she let the memories take her away.

Mackenzie walked home from school, her little sister, Paige, at her heels. The air was chillier than average on this Autumn afternoon and one could smell the coming of winter. It hung in the air and forced its way into your nostrils.

"Mackenzie!" Her sister cried out. "You're walking too fast and I can't....keep.....up!", she panted, breathlessly, her little legs working overtime.

Mackenzie stopped suddenly and spun around. Paige nearly ran into her. “Paige! You know I walk fast. I didn’t ask you to follow me home, did I?”

Just then, a small pickup truck pulled up to the curb alongside them. A familiar voice shouted, “Hey you two! You want a ride home?”

It was their older brother, Jared.

“C’mon, c’mon - I want to get home. I have a date tonight.” The door swung open and both girls climbed in beside him. Mackenzie sighed happily. She loved her brother’s truck and not just because it was his own, which was impressive all on its own, but because of the smells she associated with it: her brother’s aftershave, the musky smell of old leather seats, the faint hint of peppermint chewing gum.

"So, whatcha girls been up to?" Jared asked them, as he steered the truck down the empty sidestreets.

Mackenzie shrugged. "Not much...Say, Jared - do you think you can give me a hand with homework later?"

Jared shook his head. "Maybe...I have plans tonight. Can't any of your friends help you?"

Paige giggled. "She doesn't have any friends!"

Jared chuckled. "Wow, Paige, that was harsh! Tell you what, Mackenzie...let me see how much time it takes me to get ready for my date. I may have some time to help, ok?"

Mackenzie nodded, still glaring at her baby sister.

A few minutes later, they pulled up in front of a red brick two family flat that they called home. Jared pulled up to the curb behind a familiar looking red Chrysler.

"Shit", Jared said, the disappointment in his voice was evident. "Dad's home." Silence filled the truck.

Paige clutched her bookbag tightly to her chest. "I hope he's not drunk..."

Jared shut the truck off and slumped down in his seat. Mackenzie looked over at him. She looked up to her big brother and knew that even if dad *was* drunk, he would protect them as much as he could.

"Well, girls...I guess we should head inside. No use sitting out here, in the cold." He opened his door and got out of the truck. The girls followed suit, staying close to him as they neared the house. They entered what sounded to them like a war zone.

"Damn it, Renee! What did you do with my whiskey?", their father boomed, his thick, Irish accent slurred by cheap, Irish whiskey.

Their mother sat in an armchair, cowering in fear, her crocheting perched on her lap. "I don't know where you put it, Kieran...Maybe you drank it all."

"Damn it, woman! I'm not stupid!" He turned towards the children whose faces were filled with fear. He stormed over to Jared and grabbing him by his collar, dragged him into the middle of the living room.

"Where's it at, Jared? You been drinking my whiskey, you little bastard?"

Jared shook his head, nervously. "No.....No, dad....No. I don't drink. You know that, dad", he stammered, flinching at every sudden move his father made.

Suddenly, a shadow of rage passed over their father's face and he slapped Jared. "Don't lie to me boy!"

Mackenzie and Paige clutched tightly onto one another and they both began to cry. Their mother bounded out of her chair, threw down her crocheting, and got in between Jared and her husband.

"You leave him alone, Kieran. You're a no good drunken Irishman who blames his own mistakes on everyone else. You're no good for these children and....." Before she could finish her sentence, Kieran wheeled back and slapped her across her face, knocking her to the ground.

Jared turned to the girls, his nose bleeding. "Run! Run where no one will find you! And stay together! Go! Someone will come for you later!"

Mackenzie and Paige scrambled for the door, leaving their mother and brother to fend for themselves.

The two girls ran breathlessly down the street toward somewhere safe, anywhere safe. Midway down the block, Mackenzie stopped running, Paige following suit. They were out of breath and, not to mention, hungry. It was way past dinnertime.

Paige looked up at Mackenzie, trying to catch her breath. "What are we going to do? It's going to be dark soon!" A single raindrop landed on her face as she spoke. "And it's starting to rain!"

Mackenzie looked around feverishly, desperately. She whispered under her breath a prayer, hoping God would hear her. "Please, God, please....let us find a safe place to go." Looking up to the sky, she saw the spires of St. Joseph Catholic Church rising above the houses. "Wow, Paige. I never knew you could see our church from here." Just then, a dawn of realization came over her. "What could be more safe than a church?", she thought, grabbing her sister's hand.

"Come on, Paige. I know where we can go."

"Where?" Paige asked, excitedly.

"God's house. We'll be safe there."

CHAPTER TWO

Mackenzie immediately felt a sense of relief upon approaching the large, oak doors of St. Joseph's. She used all of her muscles to pull open the ancient doors and led Paige inside. The church was dark, lit only by candles. They walked down the center aisle and midway down, slid into a pew.

"What are we going to do, Mackenzie?" Paige asked, loudly.

Mackenzie put a finger to her lips. "Don't be so loud, Paige. This is a quiet place not meant for screaming.

We should pray. Pray that mom and Jared are ok. And most of all, pray that dad stops drinking...."

Paige kneeled down to pray. She motioned for her sister to join her. She closed her eyes and both sisters prayed silently to God.

Mackenzie looked around her. She loved this old church and looked forward to the Sunday mornings that her and her sister spent with their mother there. She breathed in deep the smells of her surroundings. Whether it was Midnight Mass on Christmas Eve or weekly Mass on Sunday mornings, the church always smelled the same to her. It was the smell of incense burning and candles lit for loved ones. It was the smell of antiquity and aging wood. It was the smell of peace. Mackenzie wanted peace to come to her family more than anything in the world. She just didn't know how to achieve it at this point in her young life.

"I wonder if God is watching us right now.", Paige whispered, shattering the silence that surrounded them.

"I'm sure he is.", an unfamiliar voice replied. The girls jumped in their seats and whirled around to see who was talking.

A young priest sat two pews behind them. He was no older than thirty with blue eyes and dark brown hair.

Mackenize stammered. "I'm sorry, Father. We didn't realize you were there."

He stood up and walked over to them, sitting in the pew directly in front of them. He turned sideways so that he could see and talk to them. "What are you girls doing here so late? It's getting dark out. Where are your parents?"

Paige stared at him inquisitively. "Where's Father McDougall? Are you new here?"

He smiled gently down at her. "Yes, I'm new here. Father McDougall is very sick and he is taking some time off." He looked to Mackenzie. "Are you two in some kind of trouble?"

Mackenzie suddenly felt nervous. She wasn't quite sure if the priest was okay with them being there, alone. She stared at him blankly.

The young priest asked again, this time much softer. "Are you girls in some kind of trouble? Do you need my help?"

Mackenzie looked at him, tears welling up in her eyes. She knew they could trust him. She knew he could help them.

"Yes." Mackenzie answered, breathlessly. "Yes, we need help, Father...."

Paige nodded excitedly. "What's your name, Father?"

He smiled at her warmly. "Anthony. Father Anthony. And what are both of your names?"

"I'm Paige and this is my sister, Mackenzie. We're hiding from our father. He's a drunk."

"Paige!" Mackenzie gasped.

"That's what mom says...." Paige argued.

Concern filled Father Anthony's face. "Did he do anything to hurt either one of you? Did he hit you?"

Mackenzie and Paige shook their heads. Mackenzie tried to explain their situation. "He gets angry when he drinks. Sometimes he gets violent, but never with us."

Father Anthony shifted uncomfortably in the pew. "Never with you, but what about your mother? Does he hit your mother? Did he hit her tonight?"

Upon hearing his question, a look of fear fell upon Mackenzie's face. "Should I tell him?", she thought. She didn't want to get her father in trouble but at the same time, she worried about her mother and hated him every time she saw him lash out at her and her brother.

As if reading her mind, Father Anthony reached out and touched her shoulder, smiling warmly at her loyalty towards her family. “Bless you, child, for being such a good, loving, loyal daughter. I only want to help you both and your family...are you both hungry? Have you had dinner?”

Paige and Mackenzie looked at one another cautiously and shook their heads.

“Well then....”, Father Anthony stood up. “Let’s get you both some food and then we can contact your family.” He grabbed both of their hands and led them down the aisle.

CHAPTER THREE

The girls sat in two over-sized armchairs facing the gigantic, oak desk that Father Anthony sat behind. He smiled at them warmly. “I'll see if Sister Margaret can bring you both something to eat.” He picked up the telephone receiver, and dialing an extension, he waited for someone to pick up the other end of the line.

“Yes....Sister Margaret. Are there any sandwiches left over from today's luncheon?...There are?.....Great! Can you be so kind as to bring a couple to my office with a couple glasses of milk?.....Yes, I have some unexpected company.....Thank you dear....Bye.” With that, he hung up the phone. He sank back into his leather chair and furrowed his brow. “So, do you girls come to Mass here every Sunday?”

Mackenzie nodded. “Yes, Father. We come with our mother and sometimes our brother, Jared.”

The young priest leaned forward. “But never with your father?”

“Right, Father. Never with daddy.”, Paige said softly. Her voice was hardly a whisper.

Father Anthony looked concerned. “Do either of you pray everyday? Do either of you pray the rosary?”

Mackenzie and Paige shook their heads.

“Prayer is a very important part of being Catholic. Especially prayer to Mary. Do you know who Mary was?”

Mackenzie and Paige both nodded. Paige giggled a little. “She was Jesus' mommy.”

Father Anthony chuckled. "Yes, Paige...She was Jesus' mommy. And she should be praised, don't you think? Your mommy should be praised also. She's been through a lot, hasn't she?"

The two girls nodded. Mackenzie looked around his office, curiously. Father Anthony had so many interesting things to look at. But Mackenzie's eyes were glued to one thing in the room: a black and white photograph of a beautiful young woman holding a little boy of about three in her arms in an ornate gold frame. Father Anthony followed her gaze to the photograph.

"I see you like that picture, Mackenzie...", he said, smiling warmly. "That's my mother and the little boy she's holding is me. She died right before I graduated high school and that's my favorite photograph of her."

"She's beautiful.", Mackenzie whispered, in a tiny voice.

Father Anthony nodded. “Yes, she was. And I adored her.” He looked longingly at the photo and then, shaking his head, sighed.

The silence was disturbed by a faint knock at the door. Sister Margaret appeared with a tray upon which two turkey sandwiches and two glasses of milk sat.

“Here you are, Father.....Oh my! What two beautiful young ladies!”

The two girls blushed. Father Anthony chuckled. “Yes, Sister Margaret. These are my dinner guests this evening.”

Sister Margaret set down the tray on a table in the corner. She smiled at the girls. “Well, aren't you lucky? I've seen you girls before, at Mass. You're always with your mother. Oh.....what *is* her name?” She pondered. “Renee! Renee O'Connor! Such a lovely, lovely woman!”

Mackenzie smiled “Thank you for the sandwiches, Sister.” Paige nodded in agreement.

“Oh, you're both very welcome. Is there anything more I can get you, Father?”

Standing up, Father Anthony nodded, walking with her towards the door. He whispered something to her and she nodded, leaving the room and closing the door behind her. Father turned back to the girls, who had moved to the table with the sandwiches on it. They were about to take the first bites out of them when Father exclaimed, “Girls! Let's thank God for what you are about to eat, yes?”

The girls put down their sandwiches, ashamed at what they were about to do. Mackenzie stammered. “I'm....I'm sorry, Father. We're just so hungry and the sandwiches look so good.”

Father Anthony smiled at her, lovingly. “I understand completely, my dear. No explanations are needed. Let's bow our heads and give thanks." He bowed his head, hands clasped before him. The girls followed suit. "Heavenly Father...Please bless the food that is before us. We ask this in Christ's name, Amen."

Paige looked up at him, innocently. "Sometimes are daddy says grace before dinner."

Father Anthony smiled. "Yes?"

Paige nodded. "But not all of the time."

Father Anthony nodded. "Well, my dear. We should remember to thank God always for what He blesses us with. Food, toys, family, friends...."

Paige smiled. "I thank God for you, Father."

Father Anthony blushed, humbled by her honesty. "Well, thank you, my dear. That means so very much to me. Now, eat up! Don't let a crumb go to waste!"

Mackenzie and Paige picked up their sandwiches and began to ravish them with great hunger and enthusiasm.

The shrill ringing of Father Anthony's phone made them jump.

"Father Anthony here....He is?......Good, send him in." He returned the phone to the cradle and smiled at the girls, watching them eat.

There was a loud knock at the door. "Come in!" Father Anthony yelled.

Jared O'Connor stepped through the door and, seeing the girls, called out, "Mackenzie! Paige!"

The girls let their sandwiches fall from their hands and ran to him, allowing themselves to be scooped up into his arms. "Mom is worried sick about you two! Have you been here all along?"

The girls nodded. Father Anthony smiled, walking over to Jared, his hand extended. "Nice to meet you, Jared. I'm Father Anthony."

Jared hugged the girls to him, ignoring Father's offer for a handshake. "Nice to meet you, Father, but we've gotta go....."

Father Anthony stepped forward momentarily and reached out to stop Jared from leaving. "Wait, Jared. Can I talk to you in the hallway a minute?"

"Yeah, sure." Jared agreed, following Father into the quiet darkness that lay outside of his well-lit office. Father Anthony closed the door quietly behind him.

"Jared....I'm concerned by the events of this evening as told to me by your two sisters."

Jared stood there, silently. His nose was swollen and had begun to turn various shades of blues and purples. He looked down at his feet, shuffling them nervously. "Father, there's nothing to be concerned about."

"Oh no?", he motioned to his nose. "How do you explain that, then?"

Jared's face felt warm, flushed with embarrassment. "Honestly, my dad gets a little out of control sometimes. But it's nothing I can't handle. Look at Mackenzie and Paige. Do they look hurt to you? I'm the one standing here with the busted nose."

"They *are* hurt, Jared....emotionally and mentally. They shouldn't have to deal with this. They're too young." He paused. "You're too young."

"You know nothing about me, Father. I can take care of this family."

Father Anthony shook his head sadly. "I want to believe you can, Jared, but...."

Jared felt anger beginning to replace his feelings of embarrassment. "Look....leave me and my family alone. Those little girls in there are fine. My mother and I are strong people and can hold our own, at the same time, making sure they're alright." Calming down, he added. "I thank you for taking care of them tonight, but that's it: one night. You won't have to worry about it again." He pushed past the young priest, throwing open the office door. "Mackenzie....Paige. Let's go. Mom's got dinner ready and you both have homework to take care of."

Mackenzie and Paige followed him out of the office and past Father Anthony. When they were almost to the exit door, Mackenzie glanced back. Father Anthony was watching them leave, with sadness in his eyes. He managed to smile at Mackenzie and wave.

Mackenzie returned the wave. She knew she would never forget him.

Later on that evening, Father Anthony prayed alone in his room. He kneeled before a statue of Mary, fingering the glass beads of his rosary gently. He usually prayed for various people that have come and gone in his life, as well as those who are still very much a part of it and not to mention for himself; for the strength and the courage to be a contradiction in a highly secular world. But tonight was different. Tonight his prayers revolved around two little girls. He knew that he was able to help them, if only their big brother realized that he was in need of help as well. "Hopefully", he thought, "I can make Jared see it before it's too late."

Mackenzie lay still in the darkness, next to her little sister, in the bed that they shared. She could hear Paige's deep breathing and she knew that she had fallen asleep. She looked up at the ceiling, trying her hardest to see through it; through this house full of sadness and into Heaven. She thought about Father Anthony. He had been so nice to them. Jared had told them not to go to the church anymore because it would only cause problems in the end. But Mackenzie couldn't help but to think how badly she wanted to go back there. And maybe she would. One day soon after school. She could always tell her mother that she had to stay after school and just go there instead. After all, she wanted to learn more about God and her faith and Mary and not to mention, prayer. "Maybe if I learned the right way to pray, God would stop daddy from drinking", she thought to herself. Mackenzie closed her eyes and before long, she was fast asleep.

CHAPTER FOUR

The next morning, at the breakfast table, Mackenzie pushed her scrambled eggs around her plate with her fork, her mind somewhere else. Her mother stared at her, a concerned look on her face. "Mackenzie, honey...don't play with your eggs, dear. They're going to get cold and cold eggs are never good."

Mackenzie mumbled. "I'm not hungry."

Her mother sighed. "Well, at least drink your juice. Jared told me about the nice young priest that took care of you girls last night. That was very nice of him."

Mackenzie's face brightened at the mention of Father Anthony. "Yes, momma, he was. He talked to us about prayer and Mary and...." Her voice trailed off as her father made his way into the kitchen.

Grabbing a cup of coffee, he sat down at the table. "Who were you just talking about, Mackenzie?"

She shrugged, afraid to tell him.

"Was it about that priest again? Paige told me about him. I don't want you to go near him...I don't trust him with my little girls."

Renee spoke up quietly. "It's not like that, Kieran...."

"Don't talk back to me, woman! They don't need to be going there, hanging out with some man. I don't care if he is a priest. They're human, they sin too." He barked.

Looking at the clock, he stood up. "I have to go to work. End of discussion." He walked out of the room, slamming the front door on the way out of the house.

Their mother stood up and began to clear the table, tears welling up in her eyes. "Momma?", Mackenzie asked in a small, quiet voice.

"Yes, dear?"

"Can you have Jared take Paige home from school today? I have to stay after to use the library...."

Her mother nodded, a faint smile on her lips. "I can do that, sweetie. Don't stay too late, ok? Try to be home before dark."

Mackenzie nodded, smiling to herself. She normally didn't lie, but this time would have to be an exception. She felt drawn back to the stillness and the peacefulness of St. Joseph's. No matter what her father said.

Father Anthony sat in the dark confessional, waiting for the next soul in search of forgiveness to come along. His mind wandered, thinking of friends and family he hadn't seen in a while. The stillness was soon disturbed by the sound of someone entering the confessional. He slid open the screened window. Whoever it was, was hidden in the shadows.

"Forgive me, Father, for I have sinned. It has been a month since my last Confession."

Father was not expecting the voice that came out of the darkness. It was a little girl. He cleared his throat. “Um....go ahead, my child.”

“Well. I lied to my mother, Father.”

“Yes, ok...about what, my dear?”

There was a long pause. “Father?”

“I’m still here....”

“Can I just talk to you a minute outside of this dark box?” Suddenly, a familiar face appeared in front of the screen.

“Mackenzie? Is that you?”

“Yes, Father.”

“Are you here with your mother and sister?”

“No....not exactly. I’m by myself.”

Father Anthony nodded, a concerned look on his face. “I’ll meet you by the pews at the front of the church. We can take a little walk.”

Her face disappeared and he heard the door to the confessional open and then close again. He said a little prayer to God to guide him when it comes to this little girl. He hadn’t had much experience dealing with females’ emotions in his lifetime; he had no sisters, only one older brother. His brother was married and he and his wife had a little girl but he only saw them on holidays.

He stood up, taking off his vestments and exited the confessional. Mackenzie was standing by the front door of the church, just as he had instructed. He walked over to her smiling. “To what do I owe this visit, Miss Mackenzie?”

She smiled. “I need to talk to you, Father. But I can’t stay too long. It will be dark soon and my mother......” She trailed off, looking down at her feet.

“Let me guess. Your mother doesn’t know you’re here?” Mackenzie nodded. “Is that what you lied to her about?” Mackenzie nodded again. Father Anthony placed a hand on her head gently. “Let’s take a walk, ok? There are gardens in the back of the church. You’ll like it there.”

Mackenzie followed the young priest as he pushed through the huge double doors and into the setting sunlight.

The gardens were some of the most beautiful that Mackenzie had ever seen. Most of the flowers had died, it being so close to winter. But that didn’t stop the birds from flying about, from tree to tree, chirping with delight.

Father Anthony looked down at Mackenzie and smiled lovingly. "So, what do you think?"

Mackenzie smiled. "I love it. I bet it's even more beautiful in the summer."

"That it is....that it is." He led her over to a tiny bench in front of a grotto which held a statue of Mary. "Now.", he said, both of them sitting down. "What brings you here, my dear?"

Mackenzie played with the hem of her skirt, wondering how to put into words what she was feeling. Father Anthony's brow furrowed. "Are you ok?"

She nodded. "I....I like it here. With you. That's why I wanted to come back. My brother and my father don't want me to, but I don't care what they think."

"And why do they not want you to come here?"

"They....they think you're bad....they say that you're only human and you sin like everyone else. That.....that you'll hurt me."

Father Anthony sighed, shaking his head. "I am only human, Mackenzie. But I would never hurt you. That's not something I would ever do. Do you believe me?"

Mackenzie nodded.

"So, what brings you here, Mackenzie? Please tell me."

"I want to learn, Father. I want to learn more about my faith. About Mary and Jesus. I want you to teach me."

Father Anthony smiled and nodded. "I think that can be arranged. But I would like to have your parents' permission to do so.....Or at the very least, your mom's."

"I think she'll be ok with it, Father. But I can have her come up here and meet you."

"Ok. Sunday after Mass. Bring her into the sacristy. You know where that is, right?"

"Yes. The room you get ready for Mass in...."

Father Anthony smiled and nodded. "Well, young lady. You should be getting home. Your parents will be worried about you." Father Anthony stood up.

Mackenzie followed suit.

"Will you be ok walking home by yourself?"

"Yes, Father. Thank you for asking." She walked with him toward the entrance to the garden.

"Have a great night, sweetie and I will see you and your mom on Sunday."

Mackenzie turned to go, smiling. She took a few steps down the path and turned around. Father Anthony was standing there, smiling at her lovingly.

Father Anthony turned to walk back into the church. "Father!" At the sound of his name, he turned, just in time to catch Mackenzie, as she ran to hug him. She squeezed him tightly. Father Anthony, still surprised, wasn't sure what to do at first. Then, slowly, carefully, he returned the hug.

"Aw, my dear, dear Mackenzie Thank you...."

"No, thank you, Father. Thank you for helping me and my sister." She pulled away from him, smiled, and ran down the path towards home.

Father Anthony walked back towards the church, breathing on his clasped hands for warmth. Sister Margaret held the door open for him. "Thank you, Sister." She nodded and smiled and began to walk away. "Sister? Did you see what just happened?"

Sister Margaret turned around. "Yes, Father, I did."

"And what do you make of it?"

"Be careful, Father."

Father Anthony looked perplexed. "Why do you say that?"

"Her father and her brother do not like you. It doesn't matter that you're a good person. You and I both know you would never hurt her. But they have this preconceived notion that you will. And don't you go thinking you can change that either!" Sister Margaret turned to go but then hesitated one last time. "Are you hungry? I can always heat up some soup from last night's dinner. We have so much left over and I would hate for it to go to waste."

Father Anthony nodded. "I would like that, Sister, thank you."

"Very well." She nodded. "Go wash up. It'll be ready before you know it." With that, she walked down the hall and into the kitchen.

Father Anthony stood alone in the foyer, thinking about what Sister Margaret had just said. Her words haunted him. Could there be truth in what she had said? As darkness began to fill the room, the warm, inviting smell of soup wafted in and found his nostrils. His growling stomach brought him out of his daydream and back into reality. Sighing, he made his way into the kitchen to wash up for dinner.

Kieran O'Connor stumbled out of the dark, smoke-filled bar and into the fresh, cool evening air. The sun was just about to sink below the horizon and the sky was filled with various shades of purples and pinks. He paused a moment to clumsily light a cigarette. He dug in his pants pockets for his car keys and, upon finding them, staggered slowly down the street, struggling to recall exactly where he had parked several hours and several glasses of whiskey ago.

Having only walked a couple feet, he gave up momentarily, sitting down on the curb. He took a long drag on his cigarette, pulling the smoke deep within his lungs. He felt the rush of the nicotine in his veins and smiled, drunkenly. "Nothing better than a Marlboro.", Kieran thought. "Unless of course, you have a Marlboro and a glass of Jameson….that's something special alright." He laughed loudly, making his head hurt. Not only was it spinning uncontrollably, but he was getting a headache to top it all off. He slumped forward and put his head in his hands, rubbing his temples slowly. He was well aware that he needed to lay off the drink. He knew that it was causing problems at home.

Kieran sighed sadly, thinking back to when he was a child and how promising life had seemed. He had hopes and dreams, things he longed to accomplish. He worked so hard and had saved up enough money so that when he turned 18 years of age, he was able to purchase a one way ticket to America. It was the best day of his life. It was the day his life had begun.

Things changed, however, upon arriving in the States. Being Irish, he was viewed as a second class citizen and the only employment he was able to obtain was work in a steel mill, just as he had back home. He still held onto those dreams and ambitions and planned on one day, taking some college classes and starting a business. Eventually, he met Renee and shortly thereafter, they were married and Jared was born. That's where his dreams were lost. He was forced to stay in the steel mill to provide for his family. And that's when the drinking started.

"Oh well…" Kieran thought. "No sense in crying over spilled milk….What's done is done." Taking another drag off his cigarette, his blurry vision happened upon the large, gothic cathedral on the opposite side of the street. It was the church that his wife and children attended. The church that he made it a point to stay away from, if at all possible. He was not a religious man, by any means. And more often than not, lately, he found himself resenting God for cursing him with this addiction. He squinted at a figure in black as it exited the large front doors of the church and sat down on the front steps, a book of some sort in his hands. Kieran grunted. It was the new, young priest that everyone seemed to have fallen in love with. "Not me…." He thought aloud. He knew what they were all about. And he didn't like it one bit. A man shouldn't be expected to live celibately. All it did was spell out "trouble". And he'd be damned if his little girls would spend two seconds alone with that man. Stumbling to his feet, he glared at the priest and made his way down the street to find his car.

Renee O'Connor separated her husband's clothes by lights and darks, getting them ready for the weekly laundry.

She hated touching his clothes. They reeked of cigarette smoke and whiskey and God forbid, whatever else he had been up to when he wasn't at home with his family. As soon as they touched her skin, she could smell the lingering stench for the rest of the day, it seemed. But nothing seemed to smell worse than the reality that was her life. Day in and day out, she cared for this man, doing everything for him short of wiping his ass. She chuckled a bit at the thought, wondering if that's what the future held. Her mind wandered back to the days when they had first married, before the children came along. It hadn't always been this bad. He was such a handsome fellow and he promised her so much. And she had believed him. God, how she had believed him. And now, after all the years of pain and heartache he had put her through, she wondered what had happened to those promises. She stuck around for the children and because, well – because she truly loved him. She winced at that thought. It was like a smack in the face. But she did. She loved him despite the drunken stumbling in at 3am…despite the fact that he spent nearly his entire paycheck at the bar and brought her home breadcrumbs with which to pay the bills……despite the beatings. She sighed, tears welling up in her eyes. The beatings were the worst. It's like he became an entirely different person when he drank. After all this time, she could still feel every single blow that had landed on her tender skin. Looking at the clock, she was shocked back to reality. It was getting late and everyone would soon be coming home for dinner. She set the laundry aside for the meantime and went into the kitchen.

CHAPTER FIVE

Renee O'Connor sat in the back pew of St. Joseph's with both of her daughters on either side of her, waiting for Mass to begin. She wasn't going to bring the girls to church today but Mackenzie had been so adamant about going and about her meeting Fr. Anthony afterward that she couldn't refuse her. She saw the excitement in her little girl's face and remembered a time long ago, when she, too, had been excited about her faith. But all of that seemed to have disappeared in recent years. It was hard for her to get out of bed most Sunday mornings. She chuckled quietly to herself. Hell - it was tough getting out of bed most mornings, let alone Sunday. Her relationship with her husband was ruined, thanks to the bottle, and after a few cracks with his belt because dinner wasn't done yet when he got home or because there was a little bit of dust on some of the furniture or just because he felt like being mean, she began to wonder why God still forced her to live anymore in this horrible existence. Where was God when she was being beat? Or when her son was beat? Or when all of the rent money and money for bills was spent in the corner bar on whiskey shot after whiskey shot? Yes, it was very obvious that she was there at Mass for her daughters' sake and for their sake only. She didn't want them to grow up hating God because she hardly believed anymore.

Her thoughts were interrupted by the sound of the organ playing the processional hymn. She grabbed Paige and Mackenzie's hands and pulled them to their feet, singing.

Mass was over as quick as it had begun. Renee and her girls remained seated in the pew, while everyone filed out around them. Soon the church was empty, save for a few people milling about, lighting candles for sick relatives or talking to old friends they hadn't seen in a while.

Mackenzie stood up eagerly. "Come on, mama. We're supposed to meet Fr. Anthony in the....the....the room where the priests get ready."

"The sacristy, my dear....the sacristy." A familiar voice broke through the silence of the church. Fr. Anthony walked up to them smiling, his hand extended towards Renee waiting for a handshake.

Renee stood up and clasped his hand in hers. “Good morning, Father...My name is Renee O’Connor.”

Father Anthony held her hand in both of his. “Very nice to meet you, ma’am. I’m Fr. Anthony.” He smiled down at Paige and Mackenzie. “You have two amazing daughters, Mrs. O’Connor, but I’m sure you know that already.”

Renee smiled and nodded. “Oh, yes....yes, I do. They are my world, Father.”

“Let’s sit down and talk. Is here in the church okay, or should we go somewhere a little more private?”

“Here is fine. Girls - why don’t you go wait in the car?”

"Or, better yet..." Father Anthony interrupted. "How about showing Paige your beautiful garden, Mackenzie? The one you were so impressed with?"

Mackenzie nodded, smiling. She stood up, and, holding the hand of her little sister, skipped off towards the door that led outside.

Fr. Anthony sat down in the pew next to Renee.

"Well, Father. I want to thank you for taking such great care of my girls the other evening. It shouldn't have been your responsibility and I appreciate it greatly."

He shook his head. "It's really not a problem. Your girls are a pleasure to be around." He looked closely at her face. There was a hint of bruising on her left cheek that she failed to hide with makeup. "How's that feeling?", he inquired, motioning towards the purple spot.

Renee blushed and looked down. Her hand came up and she gingerly touched it, wincing a bit. "It's healing.....I thought I covered the entire thing up this morning. But....I guess not."

Father Anthony looked at her with caring eyes. "Does that happen often?"

"How do I even answer that, Father? I mean, really, when you think about it, one time is way too often. It should never happen. Ever. But it does....." She paused a moment, tears welling up in her eyes. "The situation is out of control. My son, Jared, always sticks up for me and he gets the toughest of the punishment, which just isn't fair to him."

Father Anthony pulled out a handkerchief from his pocket and handed it to her.

"Thank you.", she said, taking it from him and wiping her eyes. The tears were flowing freely now and with that, the words followed. "You just don't know how tough it is! No one does! I'm trying to raise these girls to be strong and independent and self-reliable and yet, how can I possibly?"

"My father was an alcoholic, Renee. He used to come home from work, angry and bitter about how his life had turned out and he would let loose on my mother. He would use whatever he could get his hands on to beat her into submission at his feet. There was one time, however, when he grabbed the poker from the fireplace. That was when I stepped up and taught him a lesson."

Her eyes widened in surprise.

"I know what you're thinking, Mrs. O'Connor. You don't have to say a word. The day that I stood up and fought back....and I mean, truly fought back....not just took the beating for my mom....well.....that was the day he stopped his reign of terror. And that is what Jared needs to do, I'm afraid."

Renee nodded. "I'm scared for that to happen, but I agree, Father."

"And it will happen, my dear. I can promise you that. He is very protective of you and of the girls. He won't let this go on much longer. He can't. It's killing him inside." He sat back and sighed. "Now, the reason I wanted to talk to you was so that I could ask your permission."

"My permission?"

"Yes. Mackenzie wants me to teach her about her faith. Sort of like catechism. And I can make the time to do so. But I want to hear it from you. I don't want her sneaking around behind your back. That would be wrong. It could be whenever she has time during the week. Of course, school work comes first and if that starts concerning you, than no more meetings with me. And then, later on, maybe I could teach Paige, once she gets a bit older." He paused. "Tell me your thoughts."

Renee smiled and nodded. "I would like that for her, Father. Thank you for offering."

"Ok then, it's settled." He stood up. Renee followed suit. "And Mrs. O'Connor....please find comfort in the fact that God is in control. I know that the situation seems hopeless but He doesn't give us anything we can't handle. And that goes for your situation, as well. I know that it can be tough to keep on keeping on but please do and know that you are not alone. I'm here if you need me."

Renee smiled broadly, nodding. “Thank you and God bless you. It means a lot to me.”

He walked her to the side door so that she could gather her children and let them know it was time to leave. He watched them from the window as they skipped alongside their mother, giggling. A vision of his own mother flashed in his mind and just as quick as it had come, it was gone again. He turned and walked towards his office.

Monday afternoon found Father Anthony out in the garden, enjoying the cool breeze and warm sunshine, praying the Litany of the Hours quietly to himself. Sister Margaret walked out of the church and into the garden, pulling her sweater tighter to her, chilled by the cool Fall air. “Father! I’ve been looking for you everywhere!”

Father Anthony looked up from his praying. "Yes, sister? I've been out here the entire time. It's a beautiful day. Come join me." He patted the bench next to him.

Sister Margaret sat down next to him. "It's cold out here! You're going to catch your death!"

Father Anthony laughed. "Aw, dear, dear Sister....it's not as cold as you think. Besides I think I carry a little more insulation than you, if you know what I mean? Thanks to your wonderful cooking!" He patted his belly.

She shook her head laughing.

"Now...what in the world have you been looking everywhere for me for? Did I do something?"

"No, no, Father. I just wanted to talk. How did your meeting go with the little girl's mother yesterday?"

Father Anthony nodded slowly. "It went well. She told me a lot of what has been going on in their household. It's a shame, really....If I could just talk to the brother, or better yet, the father, maybe I could help in some way...Change things for them."

Sister Margaret threw her hand up to stop him from going any further. "No. You will not be their savior, Father. If the son feels threatened by you, than God only knows how the father would react. It's not a good situation. And you should stay out of it as much as possible." She could see the sadness wash over his face. "Teach the girl....fill her heart and her mind with God. But that's it. Keep your self separate from what's going on in their home. Let God handle that."

Father Anthony nodded. "I know you're right."

The aging nun stood up, straightening out her dress. She pulled her rosary from her pocket and wrapped it around her hand. "Well, I'm going inside. It's much too cold out here and besides, I need to say my rosary. Please don't stay out here too long. And please think about what I've said." She turned and walked back towards the church.

CHAPTER SIX

Monday evening, after dinner, Renee was cleaning off the table and gathering the dishes to be washed with the help of Mackenzie and Paige.

Jared sat watching them for a moment and then, pushing himself away from the table, he cleared his throat. "Paige.....Mackenzie.....go run and play. I want to talk to mom alone for a bit."

The two girls stopped what they were doing and looked from Jared and back to their mother.

"Go on girls - you heard your brother. Go run your bath water."

Hesitating, the girls put down their dish towels and ran upstairs. Renee put the last of the dishes in the sink and turned around to face Jared, wiping her hands with the towel. "Is something wrong, son?", she inquired.

Jared stared at her a moment longer. "I saw you coming out of the church yesterday with Mackenzie and Paige but it was after Mass had been over a while.....Is something wrong?"

Renee shook her head, looking down at her feet. She looked back up at Jared. "No....nothing wrong." Her voice quavered.

"So, why did it take you all so long to leave after Mass?"

“Well, we were talking to Father Anthony. It seems that Mackenzie has really taken a liking to him and wants to learn about the faith from him.....sort of like Catechism. Remember when you used to go to Catechism, Jared? Oh, you were so cute and so little then....”

“Mom....” Jared cut her off mid-sentence. “That was a long time ago.”

Renee smiled. “Yes dear but you were so eager to learn.....”

“Enough, mom! That was before I realized that the entire religion is a farce! God doesn’t exist! At least not in this family he doesn’t!”

Renee gasped, clasping the gold crucifix that hung from her neck with shaking hands. “Jared, no! Don’t say such things!”

Jared shook his head with anger and frustration. "No, mom....stop living a lie! I can't believe you're allowing Mackenzie to spend time alone with a grown man learning about a faith that doesn't exist! God only knows what he's filling her head with!"

Renee moved closer to Jared, her hand held out before her, wanting to touch him, to calm him, like she used to be able to when he was a baby. But he was her baby no longer. He resembled his father when he got angry. It scared her. "Jared, please....Let's sit down and talk about this.....you're flying off the handle....."

"Damn it, mom! You're so blind! Why can't you see that religion does nothing but fill your heart with false hope?" Jared pushed past her, nearly knocking her down. "This family is hopeless! Hopeless! I can't stand living here!" Turning to leave, he punched the wall, causing a framed picture of Jesus to crash to the ground, the glass frame shattering, scattering glass shards everywhere.

Renee stood in the middle of the kitchen, hands shaking uncontrollably. She sat down in a chair and putting her head in her hands, began to cry.

Jared raced down the residential street in his truck, clutching the steering wheel with angry hands. The fall leaves littered the street, making the road slippery. Upon reaching the intersection he turned the corner a little too quickly and caused the tail end of the truck to fish tail. Getting the automobile back under control, Jared sighed loudly. "I'd better take it easy," he thought. "Don't need a ticket or, worse yet, an accident on my record."

A few minutes later, he had reached his destination. He eased the truck into the church parking lot and into a parking spot near the door. The lot was empty, save for himself.

Hopping out of the car, he reached under his seat, pulling out his late grandfather's missalette, which was a gift to him when he passed away. Jared kept it there for the times when he needed to get away and pray. This was one of those times.

He walked up to the massive oak doors and tried to pull one open. It was locked. He tried the other one. That was locked as well. "That's odd," he thought. "These doors are always open."

Jared walked around to the side of the church. He was losing daylight rapidly and it was getting colder and colder by the minute. He walked through the garden and up to the side door. Peering through the glass, he wasn't able to see any signs of life. He tried knocking. No answer. Jared waited for a few minutes more and then decided to leave. As he was walking away, he heard the door open behind him. He whirled around to see Father Anthony.

"Can I help you?" Father Anthony inquired, peering into the darkness.

Jared cleared his throat. "I'm sorry to bother you, Father....I tried the front doors and they were locked...." He walked closer to the priest and further into the light cast by the inner hallway of the church.

Father Anthony recognized him at once. He wasn't sure whether to be happy to see him or suspicious of his presence. "Oh....Jared, right? What can I help you with?"

"I just wanted to come inside and pray. Just spend some time with the Lord. But I can totally understand if the church is closed for the night." He pulled his jacket tighter around himself and sniffled. The cold air was making his nose run.

Father Anthony paused a moment, trying to assess the situation. He seemed sincere enough, why not let him in? He stepped back, holding the door open a little wider. "Come on in..."

Jared nodded and brushed past Father Anthony and into the dimly lit hallway.

"How much time do you need, Jared? I want to be able to lock up behind you when you leave."

"Is a half hour too much, Father? I don't want to keep you...."

Father Anthony shook his head vehemently. "Not at all, not at all. I have plenty of work to keep me busy in my office. Stuff that I've fallen behind on in the past few weeks because of other.....other engagements."

Jared frowned a little, remembering at once why he had been so upset tonight. "A lot of work, huh? Tell me, Father....how do you have time, then, to spend afternoons with my little sister?"

"Well, she's very special and I don't mind helping her out....."

Jared gripped his missalette tighter. "I still don't understand, *Father*.", he said sarcastically. "How do you possibly have time for her? And you don't have to tell me she's special....I already know this...."

Father Anthony shook his head, his brow furrowing. "Wait, Jared. You're misunderstanding me."

"No. I think I understand just fine", he interrupted. Jared moved closer to the priest. He pounded a pointing finger into his chest. "Don't - you - hurt - her." He emphasized each word, hoping it got through to Father Anthony.

Father Anthony stepped backwards, a sick feeling in the pit of his stomach. "I think you should leave. I think you've stayed long enough."

Jared's face turned red with anger. He pushed Father Anthony backwards, gently but threateningly. "Don't you get any ideas in your head....like calling the cops. I didn't set out to cause trouble with you. But I defend my own, do you understand me? I protect them from all harm...not just from my father."

Father Anthony clutched his fists. He didn't appreciate feeling intimidated. Trying to calm the situation down, he put his hands up. "Look, Jared...I surrender. I mean no harm to anyone in your family. And I'm saddened by the fact that you feel that way....I mean, you don't even know me and you accuse me falsely....How can I prove to you that I mean no harm? I know a fight is what you want, but no fight will you get from me."

Jared stepped back, a defeated look on his face. He opened and closed his fists, looking down at the ground. After what seemed like an eternity, he looked up at the priest. Father Anthony was surprised to see the look of embarrassment mixed with sadness spread across his face. "Oh my God, Father....I am so sorry. Please don't call the cops....please don't tell my father....he'll kill me.....", he panicked, near tears.

Father Anthony sighed, relieved that he had finally come to his senses. "No, no....I won't tell anyone. This is between you and I. Come on - let's go sit and talk in the church. It's peaceful in there at night and maybe you'll be able to unload some of your burdens." Putting his arm around the teenage boy, the priest led him into the dark, cool church and to a pew in the back.

Jared sat down with a sigh. He was suddenly exhausted - mentally and physically. He looked up at the giant crucifix that hung above the altar. Oh, how he missed the way things used to be in his family. "You know, Father....we used to hang out all the time, my dad and I. We used to go fishing and throw the football around in the backyard....He taught me how to throw a perfect spiral. But now....." He choked on his last words and bent forward, his head in his hands. He had begun to cry.

Father Anthony put a hand gently on his shoulder. “It’s ok....let it go....you need to let it go. This shouldn’t be your burden. You shouldn’t have to be the hero, protecting everyone. You’re still a kid yourself, Jared.”

Jared looked up, tears streaming down his face. “I want to let it go, Father. But my mom.....and my little sisters.....I’m so afraid for them.”

“When did all of this start? The abuse?”

Jared thought a moment. “Right after I was born. He had to get a better job and so he was forced into the steel factory. Following in my grandfather’s footsteps, you know?....steel was in his family’s bloodline back in Ireland.” Father Anthony nodded. “Only that’s not what he wanted to do. He comes home so tired every night. It’s hard work, you know? Pounding steel. Finally, he snapped, I guess. One night, we were all sitting around in the living room, my mom and sisters and I....and we were starving. There was nothing in the house to eat. And we knew that he was getting paid and we'd be able to get food." Jared stopped a moment and shook his head, his eyes glazed over. "But he didn't come right home from work. Mom was so worried. Me and the girls had fallen asleep with our stomachs rumbling. But that sleep didn't last long....At 1:00 AM, he came stumbling in, crashing into the coffee table, knocking over mom's knick-knacks. Drunk. A belly full of whiskey. Mom asked him where he'd been and where his paycheck was." He paused, shaking his head.

"And what did he say?"

"He gave her five dollars.....told her that was all that was left. Told her to buy some groceries and pay some bills. And then beat the hell out of her because there wasn't a hot meal waiting for him."

Father Anthony shook his head angrily. "My God! What if I call Child Protective Services, Jared? I could do it anonymously....no one would ever know it was me...."

Jared interrupted quickly. "No! All they will do is separate us....we can't be apart, my sisters and I. We're a family and that's how we'll stay." He stood up and backed out of the pew and into the main aisle. "Look, I appreciate you trying to help, I really do. But I don't want to do anything that will tear this family apart....Please understand that."

Father Anthony nodded and stood up. "I understand. I'm just in a very difficult position. I don't want to see any of you hurt. It kills me."

Jared nodded. “Thank you. For everything. And I’m sorry I ever judged you.” He walked towards the door, the young priest following. “I have to get going. I’ve got school in the morning.”

Father Anthony nodded, opening the door for Jared. “Take care and I’m here anytime you need to talk.”

Jared managed a weak smile and, pulling his coat tightly shut, walked out into the blustery night air.

Jared got home a short while later. All of the lights were off in the house and his dad’s car was in the drive-way. “I hope they’re sleeping.”, Jared thought as he made his way to the porch. “I cannot deal with his crap tonight.”

Unlocking the door to the house, he quietly and carefully made his way inside. It was quiet and dark throughout. Stumbling through the darkness, he noticed a dark form laying on the couch. "It has to be dad", he thought. "I really hope I don't wake him up."

No sooner did the thought cross his mind, his father sat up and said groggily. "Wha...?? Who.....who's there??"

"It's me, dad. Jared. Why don't you go onto bed? The couch can't be that comfortable and you don't want your back to hurt tomorrow."

Kieran sat up, rubbing his head. He reached over and turned the lamp on. Shielding his eyes from the light, he looked Jared up and down. "It's a school night, Jared. Why aren't you in bed? Everyone's sleeping but you."

Jared stammered nervously. "I had some research to do at the library. Got a project I'm working on...." He was staring at his father, trying to determine his level of drunkenness.

Kieran sighed. "Fine, fine." He held up an empty glass that was sitting on the end table. "Do me a favor, kiddo, and get your dad some more of the ole' Jameson, will ya? I'm so thirsty and it seems as if I'm fresh out...."

Jared reached out and took the glass from his father. "Dad...it's late. Why don't you just call it a night. Just go to bed....with mom...."

Kieran quickly stood up and grabbed ahold of Jared's arm with a grip so tight it made his son let out a yelp. "Don't you argue with me, boy." He was wide awake now. ""Do you understand me? You aren't the man in this house. You are nothing but some punk kid trying to piss his father off." He lessened his grip some. "Mom told me what happened earlier between you and her and that's why I've been waiting up for you." His eyes narrowed, his brow furrowing. "You disrespecting your mother, boy? Who the hell do you think you are?"

Jared cowered. "No one...I don't think I'm anyone. I'm....I'm sorry, dad....."

Kieran let go of his son, shoving him backwards. "Your mother deserves the apology, not me. And you can clean up that mess in the kitchen. The one you made earlier. There's glass all over the floor." He started to walk towards the bedroom. Turning around, he walked back to Jared and got close to his face. "I can smell your fear. You're no son of mine." He sneered at the fearful look on his son's face and then stumbled into the bedroom, slamming the door behind him.

Jared stood in the living room, frozen, shaking and near tears. He couldn't help the fear; his father knew how to push his buttons and therefore keep him afraid and helpless. He wanted so badly to stand up to him and wondered why he wasn't strong enough to do so as of yet. What would it take? He almost didn't want to know the answer to that question.

Breathing deeply, the fear subsiding a bit, he walked slowly into the kitchen, turning on the light. Shattered glass covered the floor. The picture of Jesus lay in its frame on the table, salvaged no doubt by his devoted mother. Jared picked up the frame and, with his finger, traced the outline of the glowing halo that surrounded Jesus' head. Tears welling up in his eyes, he whispered, "I do believe, Lord....please know that....."

"He knows that, son...he knows."

Jared whirled around, startled. There his mother stood, hair messed up and eyes groggy from sleep and swollen from crying. "Momma.....I'm.....so......sorry.", he stammered, the tears streaming down his face.

She held out her arms to him and embraced him. She closed her eyes and suddenly he was her baby boy again. "There, there....no worries. I understand your frustration and anger. I understand and more importantly, He understands. He sees what you have to deal with on a daily basis. He knows."

"I hope so, momma. Everything I said to you, I take back. Everything I said to you, I don't mean...."

"I know, I know.", Renee said, reassuringly. "Where did you run off to tonight?"

Jared pulled back, wiping his eyes with the back of his hands. "I went to talk to God....I went to St. Joseph's....."

Renee nodded, smiling. "Yes. I figured as much."

Jared chuckled. "Yeah, yeah...sure you did!" His smile faded as quick as it had appeared. "Seriously though, Ma....I went there looking for God but found a friend."

"Father Anthony?"

Jared nodded. "Yes....he's such a great guy. I totally see him in a different light now. The girls are in good hands with him....But...." He lowered his voice to a whisper. "Don't tell dad about it, ma. He won't like it. He won't understand."

Renee nodded. "I know, Jared. I know."

"Alright. I'm going to sweep up this glass and get to bed. Morning comes early. I'll replace that frame, ma. I promise."

Renee nodded, hugging him good night. Quietly, she shuffled off to bed. Jared stood there a moment longer, thinking about the day's events and after finishing up sweeping, he followed suit.

CHAPTER SEVEN

The next day after school, Mackenzie and Paige walked towards home, their backpacks bouncing around behind them. When they had reached the corner that St. Joseph's sat on, Mackenzie stopped suddenly.

"Alright, Paige....I have to go inside the church now. You can go on home without me."

The look on Paige's face was one of confusion. "What are you talking about? Come on, let's go home! We're missing the Bugs Bunny on tv....."

Mackenzie shook her head. "No, Paige. I'm meeting with Father Anthony today. Every day. After school."

Paige shook her head. "Mommy didn't tell me anything about that. Does she know?"

Mackenzie nodded, walking backwards towards the church. "Be careful and look both ways! We'll play Barbies later, I promise." Smiling and waving, she turned and ran up to the front door of the church. She pulled it open slowly and disappeared inside.

Paige turned around and began walking towards home. "Why couldn't I meet with Father Anthony?", she thought, as she trudged along. It just wasn't fair. As she rounded the corner and onto the block where she lived, her pace quickened. She didn't want to be late for Bugs Bunny.

Nearing home, her jealousy of Mackenzie was already forgotten.

A few minutes later, Paige rushed through the front door, the screen door slamming behind her.

"Damn it, Paige! How many times have I told you not to slam that door?" Her father sat on the sofa, reading the newspaper.

"Sorry, daddy. Bugs Bunny is on!!" She grabbed the remote control and flopped down indian style in front of the tv.

Kieran snickered, folding the paper back to its original shape. Renee walked into the room, drying her hands on a dish towel. "Paige....take off your coat and backpack. Silly girl!" She reached down and helped her.

Her precious daughter was unshakeable when Bugs Bunny was on.

Kieran shook his head, smiling. “Where’s Mackenzie?”

Renee answered nervously. “Oh....she’s at the library, doing some extra homework. Extra credit, I think.”

Paige whirled around. “No, she’s not, Mommy. She’s at St. Joseph’s with Father Anthony. I thought you knew that....”

Kieran frowned. “What? Is she telling the truth, Renee?”

Renee glared at Paige. “Well - um - yes she is.”

“Why would you lie to me like that?”

"He's a good man, Kieran. And he has nothing but good intentions towards your daughter. Please stop overreacting."

"Overreacting?" Kieran stood up suddenly and threw down his newspaper. "Woman....you knew how I felt about this and, still, you allow it to continue. That's it...." He stomped to the hall closet, snatched his coat off its hanger and headed for the front door.

Renee ran to the door ahead of him, trying to prevent him from leaving. "No, Kieran, stop! I can't let you do this!"

"Woman, get out of my way. I'm going to go pick my daughter up. She's in the hands of a stranger and that doesn't sit well with me at all."

Renee stepped aside hesitantly.

"It shouldn't sit well with you either, Renee. And you call yourself a "good mother"? Maybe you should rethink that." Pulling open the front door, he slammed it behind him, trudging across the lawn to the driveway. Hopping into his car, he sped out onto the deserted street and towards the church.

Mackenzie and Father Anthony sat at the small table in his office, a book of saints opened before them. "So....even I can become a saint someday, Father?", Mackenzie asked, her wonder-filled voice nearly a whisper.

Father Anthony smiled. "Yes, my dear. We all have an opportunity to live as saints during our lives."

"Does that mean that I shouldn't hit my sister anymore?"

Father Anthony laughed. "Well - yes. Do you think you should be hitting her in the first place, Mackenzie?"

Mackenzie thought for a moment. "Well, I guess not." She paused a moment more. "But what if she deserves it?"

Father Anthony stood up, stretching. He smiled down at Mackenzie. "No, my dear. Not even then. Are you thirsty? I think Sister Margaret is making some fresh lemonade and I could have her bring us a glass."

Mackenzie nodded enthusiastically. "Oh yes, Father. I would love some."

"Lemonade it is then....coming right up!"

Father Anthony stepped out into the hallway, closing the door quietly behind him. He was just about to head down the hallway to the kitchen when heard a loud pounding on the side entrance door. He stopped in his tracks, momentarily frozen, wondering who it could be. He wondered for a second if he had forgotten to cancel an appointment - perhaps with an engaged couple preparing for Holy Matrimony or from another abused wife, not knowing who to turn to. The steel industry was a tough business and it had broken many men, leaving them unfixable.

He walked to the door slowly. The loud pounding shattered the silence again. He started to get a little angry. The church building was old and so was the door; he doubted it could take much more abuse.

Father Anthony flung the door open. In front of him stood a red-haired, blue-eyed Irishman, hands balled into fists, his face full of wild fury. He was breathing heavily as if he had just ran from where it was he came.

"Mackenzie.....", he growled. "I've come for Mackenzie."

Father Anthony tried to diffuse the situation with a smile. He held out his hand. "You must be her father? It's very nice to meet you! My name is Father Anthony...."

Kieran cut him off rudely. "I know who you are. And I knew what you mean to do, sir. Kindly step aside and let me go find my daughter."

Father Anthony was dumbstruck. "If you would just take a moment and we can discuss things....you're overreacting, Mr. O'Connor."

Kieran sneered at the young priest. "Back in Ireland, Father, we have a different way of "discussing" things....", his accented words rolled heavily off of his tongue, "......we use our fists, lad....much more productive."

He stepped closer towards the young priest. He held a scarred hand up to Father Anthony. "See these scars? I didn't get 'em on the assembly line banging out parts...." Kieran stepped back, smiling. "Now, where's my daughter?"

Father Anthony stepped aside and motioned to his office. "She's in there."

Kieran stormed past Father Anthony and threw open the office door. "Let's go, Mackenzie....it's time for dinner and mother's worried sick about you."

Mackenzie, shaking with fear, pushed her chair back from the table and slowly walked towards her father.

"Come on, girl! Get a move on!" He grabbed her hand and pulled her out into the hallway and towards the side entrance where he had come in. He shoved her out into the cold night air and turned to face the priest. "You leave her be. Go ahead and molest any other family's children. But you leave her and Paige alone....or next time our meeting will not be as civilized...." Storming out into the cold, he slammed the door behind him.

Father Anthony stood there, staring at the door for what seemed like an eternity.

"What in God's name is going on out here?" Sister Margaret stood in the doorway to the kitchen, wiping her hands on a dishtowel. "Are you alright? What happened?"

Father Anthony nodded, turning to face her. "Yes, Sister. Everything's okay." He tried to smile but he wore his heart on his sleeve. His face was a wide open book for anyone who chose to read it.

Sister Margaret shook her head. "No - I don't believe you. Not for one second. Look at you! You're.....you're shaking! And you're white as a ghost...." She began to walk towards him slowly.

Father Anthony held up his hand, hoping she would stop and not come any closer. "It's....nothing, Sister.", he stammered. He walked to the door of his office. "I want to be alone now....no dinner for me. I'm....I'm sorry. I hope you'll understand and forgive me...."

"Certainly, Father." Sister Margaret softly replied.

"Thank you." He entered his office and quietly shut the door.

Father Anthony awoke in the middle of the night with a start. He sat up in his bed, gasping for air. He looked around the dark room, making sure he was alone. The dream had felt so real; it had really startled him. In it, he had relived the evenings happenings, only Mr. O'Connor was replaced with his father. He leaned over and switched on the bedside lamp. A soft, warm glow filled the room. Looking down, he was shocked to see his nightshirt soaked with sweat. "My God! What in the world?"

Getting out of bed, he crossed the room and pulled a clean t-shirt out of a dresser drawer. Pulling off the wet nightshirt, he put the clean, dry one on. Flipping on the hall light, he carefully plodded downstairs to the kitchen. Opening the refrigerator, he examined its contents. "Warm milk? Or something stronger?", he thought. He opted for the latter.

He opened the cupboard above the refrigerator and pulled out a half empty bottle of scotch. Grabbing himself a glass, he poured himself a half glass, paused a moment, and then, shrugging, filled the glass up the rest of the way. "It has been a while.", he thought to himself. "I deserve a bit of a break...."

Father Anthony slowly sipped on the scotch, savoring the deep, rich flavor of it. He loved it; loved the way it made him feel. The warmth radiated from his toes up to the top of his head. In the past, prior to the priesthood, he had discovered that he enjoyed alcohol a bit too much for his comfort. He could see how easy it would be to slip under its spell. And it frightened him. It reminded him of his own father. And that was something that he vowed to never let happen.

And so he stopped. Cold turkey. Never looking back. Until recently. That bottle began to speak to him again. Up until tonight, he had been strong enough to resist. But the events of that evening had shaken him to his very core and left him feeling entirely too unstable.

Father Anthony spent the rest of the night there at his kitchen table, alone with his bottle of scotch. By the time the sun began to rise, he had finished the bottle off and had stumbled drunkenly back to bed.

CHAPTER EIGHT

Father Anthony was awakened late the next morning by the ringing phone and the unseasonably warm sunshine penetrating his bedroom window and illuminating his face. He tried to sit up quickly but his pounding head cried out to him. He let out a groan and, leaning over the side of the bed, snatched the phone from its cradle.

"Hello?", he grumbled softly.

"Father! Where in the world have you been? Do you know what time it is?"

Father Anthony glanced at the clock. 12:59 PM. "Yes, Sister....I know what time it is. Is there something you need?"

"Well, yes", Sister Margaret said, concern filling her voice. "You had morning appointments that I had to cancel because I couldn't find you anywhere."

He groaned again, running a hand through his hair. "I'm sorry, my dear. I will be down in my office shortly. I.....I must have overslept."

"Ok, Father. I'll make some coffee for you." There was a click and then a dial tone.

Sighing, he managed to pull himself out of bed and stumble to the bathroom. Flipping on the light, he caught a glimpse of himself in the mirror: unshaven, hair ruffled, bloodshot eyes. A mess. He grabbed hold of the scapular around his neck and prayed silently. After the events of the night before, he knew that he needed God to be with him more than ever before.

Turning on the water in the shower to full force, he stepped out of his clothes and stepped in, shutting the curtain behind him, hoping that the hot water would wash away his uncleanliness, both inside and out.

It was late afternoon when Father Anthony finally found his way into his office. While opening the blinds to let the midday sun in, he caught a glimpse of something on the floor by the table. He walked over to it and, bending down, he picked up a small pink backpack. It was Mackenzie's. He knew he would have to return it to her.

Sister Margaret knocked softly on the door frame. "I have your coffee, Father....Just made it fresh.....Figured you would need it."

He looked up from the backpack and smiled weakly. Setting it down on the table, he walked over and took the mug from her. "Thank you for being so faithful, Sister. You don't know how much that means."

She nodded, eyeing him curiously. "Is that Mackenzie's backpack?"

"Yes."

She cleared her throat. "Well, Father.....I could take it to her house later, if you'd like...."

Father Anthony took a deep breath. Holding it for a moment, he regarded the backpack, a painful look crossing his face. "No.....I will do it."

“But, Father......after last night.....”, Sister Margaret began to argue her case.

“Sister, stop this instant! My head is throbbing, my stomach is turning, and all you want to do is lecture me?”, he yelled, clenching his fists in frustration.

“I.....I’m sorry.” Sister Margaret took a step back. She was shocked to see such anger from such a normally peaceful man.

Realizing how uncalled for his outburst had been, he reached out to her, and, touching her arm, began to smile.

“No...it’s me who’s sorry, Sister. I had no right yelling at you like that. It’s just that....well, I made my bed and now I must lie in it. I brought all of this on myself. And I need to face it head on.”

Sister Margaret nodded. “I’ll leave you alone. Enjoy your coffee.” She turned around and left his office, closing the door behind her.

Sitting down at the table and taking a long sip of his coffee, Father Anthony reflected on the night’s events. The anger he felt toward Mr. O’Connor for assuming that just because he wore a collar, it meant he was a pedophile. The pain he felt when he let Mr. O’Connor bully him; the memories of his own father felt like fresh wounds again, as if someone ripped open the stitches, revealing the unhealed sore below. And most of all, it bothered him how he had dealt with that anger and pain; drinking to the point of blacking out was not something he was proud of. It was a side of himself that he thought was long forgotten. It was a side of himself that he should have buried along with his father.

He touched the backpack, tears filling his eyes. Sighing, he stood up. Shrugging on his coat, he picked up the backpack and walked out the door.

Mackenzie sat at the kitchen table, Jared next to her, trying her best to learn long division. Jared sighed. "Mackenzie. You're making this more difficult than it needs to be...."

Mackenzie shook her head. "I just don't get it. Mom - can't I just go out to play till dark? I can do my homework later.....", she whined.

Renee was at the stove, stirring a pot of chili. Setting down the spoon, she turned to face her daughter. "Absolutely not. Homework comes first. Besides, there's not much more than an hour or so of daylight left. And dinner will be read before you know it."

Mackenzie sulked, sliding down in her chair. Crossing her arms, she began to pout. "Whatever...."

Just then, there was a loud knock at the front door. Paige, who was done with her homework and watching cartoons, hopped off the couch and ran to the door. Throwing it open, she squealed with surprise and delight. "Oh!! Father Anthony! Momma.....it's Father Anthony!"

Renee walked into the living room, wiping her hands on a dish towel, Mackenzie and Jared following behind. "Come in, Father! You'll catch a cold out there!"

Father Anthony looked around carefully. He hadn't seen Mr. O'Connor's car in the driveway so he wasn't sure if he was home.

"It's ok, Father...." Mackenzie smiled. "Daddy's still at work."

Renee nodded. "Please come in and grace us with your company. Even if it's only for a few minutes."

Father Anthony smiled and stepped inside. He was holding something behind his back. "Well....I appreciate that. Mackenzie seemed to have forgotten something last night. She and her father left so quickly...." He pulled out the pink backpack.

Mackenzie's face lit up with joy. "My backpack!!"

Renee smiled. "Oh, thank you, Father! She couldn't remember what she had done with it. She thought she might have left it in her daddy's car." She shut the door behind the priest. "Would you like to stay for dinner? We're having chili.....it's just about done....."

Father Anthony shook his head sadly. "Oh, thank you, my dear. But I don't think I should...."

"It's really ok, Father. Kieran isn't due home for another few hours.....He never comes right home from work. We would love your company."

Mackenzie begged him to stay. "Please, Father. My momma makes the best chili."

Father Anthony chuckled. "Well then....the best chili? How can I argue with that?"

Renee helped him with his coat, taking it and hanging it up in the hall closet. Jared walked up to Father Anthony, his hand outstretched. "Hello, Father. It's nice to see you again."

"Same here, Jared. Been taking care of these beautiful women, I see. Everyone's so vibrant!"

The girls blushed, giggling. Renee rolled her eyes and laughed.

"I'm trying, Father.....", Jared said. "I'm trying."

They all sat down to dinner a short while later. In between bites of chili, Father Anthony shared humorous stories with them, making them laugh and easing their minds for the meantime.

Renee was just finishing up dishes when she heard a car door slam shut. She looked over to Jared, a terrified look on her face. "Is that? No...it can't be."

Father Anthony stood up from the table.

"Please sit down, Father. You're our guest. You have every right to be here." Renee pleaded with him.

He slowly sat back down, an uneasy look on his face.

Renee walked to the living room, wringing her hands nervously.

Kieran opened the front door, bringing in with him a cool breeze. He held a half empty bottle of whiskey in his hand. Drunkenly fumbling with his coat, he looked up to see his wife staring at him from the doorway of the kitchen for the first time. "Renee.....who's car is that parked in front of our house? Who's visiting at this time of night? One of Jared's friends?"

Renee shook her head. "Are you hungry? Dinner's ready...."

Setting the bottle down on the end table, Kieran flopped down in his recliner, trying to pull his work boots off without untying them. He sighed heavily and sat back in his chair, giving up on the boots for now. He was a little annoyed with his wife's answer. Why wouldn't she answer the question, for Christ's sake?

"Renee....", he said, the impatience in his voice slowly rising. "Answer my question, woman. Who's car is that?"

Father Anthony appeared in the doorway behind Renee. "It's mine, Mr. O'Connor. I was just returning Mackenzie's backpack. She left it in my office last night."

Kieran clumsily climbed to his feet, nearly knocking over the table lamp. "I thought we agreed that you are not to go anywhere near my daughter again? I thought we had an agreement?"

Father Anthony moved towards the coat closet. "I mean no harm, Mr. O'Connor....I was just leaving."

"What are you trying to do, Father?", Kieran growled angrily. "Are you trying to take my place in this house? With my family? Are you trying to get rid of me?" He stepped closer to Father Anthony, his hands balled into fists.

Father Anthony stepped back, holding his hands up in front of him. "Now, wait....You're drunk and I don't think you know what you're saying....But let's try and be rational here...."

"To hell with your rationality. To hell with you." He paused, looking towards the kitchen. "Where's the girls, Renee? Send them upstairs...."

Renee called for Mackenzie and Paige and rushed them up into their room. She could see the fear on their faces. It broke her heart.

Kieran stepped closer still to the young priest. "You know, my boy, when I showed you the scars on my hands last night, that was a warning. Where I'm from, in Dublin, we let our fists speak for us....we don't have all of the fancy words you priests do...."

Father Anthony shook his head. "Mr. O'Connor, I don't think you give yourself enough credit...."

"Don't interrupt me....You have no earthly clue about me. All you priests, you judge us. Sending us straight to hell. But, I'll be damned if you do that to me...."

"Leave him alone!"

Kieran turned to see Jared standing in front of his mother. His eyes were alive with fury. Kieran laughed. "Oh, holy mother of God! You know, Jared...you can act like a big brave man all you want, but you still reek of fear....you will never be better than me, boy, so quit trying...."

Jared shook his head. "You can't push me around anymore....I'm stick of living like this. You're no good."

Father Anthony interjected. "Jared......Mr. O'Connor.....let's just sit down and talk. A peaceful solution is needed here."

"Stay out of this.....", Kieran snapped, a drunken grin spreading across his face. "This is between me and my boy now. Or is it Jared? Why are you protecting this pedophile? Did he touch you too?"

Bracing himself, Jared's right fist exploded against his father's jaw, knocking him backwards to the ground. He fell onto him, his fists flying and connecting in a fit of rage.

For what seemed like an eternity, Jared remained on top of his father, pummeling him with all of his might, trying to make him hurt as much as he had made his mother and sisters hurt. Violence was the only language that his father spoke fluently.

Somewhere, in the distance, he could hear his mother screaming. But all he could focus on was his father.

Suddenly, he felt hands lift him off of his father. He was set down hard on the floor, his fists still flying, only now, connecting with nothing.

“Stop it!” He could hear a familiar voice yell. A man’s voice. Father Anthony. “For the love of God, stop it!”

Snapping out of the maniacal rage that overcame him, Jared stopped swinging and lay back onto the floor, exhausted and out of breath. His fists were cut and bloodied and his heart raced. He heard sirens getting closer and closer to the house. He looked to his mom who was kneeling near her husband, crying. At once, Jared knew she must have called the police. He began to cry.

“Oh, Jared.....I just had to. I thought you were going to kill each other!”, he heard her cry. “Oh, Kieran....Please be ok.....I never wanted things to end up this way.....”

Kieran moaned. His face had begun to turn all different shades of blues and purples. His lips were swollen and busted and his nose was crooked and bleeding. He knew that it was broken.

A matter of minutes after the sirens stopped, their deafening shrill piercing the cool night air, there was a loud knock at the door.

Father Anthony opened it quickly and ushered the two policemen inside.

"What seems to be the problem here? Looks like there was a bit of a brawl, huh, Padre?"

Father Anthony nodded. "Yes, officer. I think he's hurt pretty bad."

The officer nodded and used his radio to call for an ambulance. The second policeman bent over Kieran. "Hey buddy....can you hear me?" He snapped his fingers a few times. "Can you hear me?"

Kieran moaned and tried to speak. His lips were too swollen and cut for anything intelligible to find its way out.

"Ok, ok....relax. An ambulance is on it's way." The officer turned to Jared. "Is this your dad?"

Jared nodded, tears still streaming down his face. "Y....yes, officer....", he stammered.

The policeman frowned, shaking his head. "Man oh man....don't you two know that a father and son aren't supposed to beat up on each other?"

"Momma?", a small voice whispered, full of fear. "Is daddy ok?"

Renee turned to see Mackenzie and Paige, standing at the foot of the stairs in their nightgowns. "Yes, baby....now both of you....run off to bed....." Hesitantly, they turned and ran up the stairs.

The policeman took out his notepad. “Ma’am....I know you’re upset but I need to ask you a few questions. Do you think your husband will want to press charges?”

Renee shrugged hopelessly, tears streaming down her face. “I honestly don’t know....” She walked to where Jared sat and, upon sitting down next to him, she embraced him lovingly. “You gotta understand that my husband had been drinking.....that he provoked my son....one too many times.....”

The officer nodded, making notes on his paper. “I need to get a statement from each one of you....”

Father Anthony spoke up. “Can you hear mine first? I really need to get back to the church.”

“Not a problem, Father. Let’s step outside.”

Taking his coat from the closet, Father Anthony walked over to Jared. He kneeled down next to him. He took the boy's face in his hands. "You be strong.....you hear me? Everything will be ok....trust me."

Jared nodded, a faint smile making a brief appearance on his lips.

Standing up and touching Renee gently on her head, he followed the policeman outside, just as the ambulance was pulling up in the driveway.

CHAPTER NINE

A month later, as the first snow of the winter fell softly to the ground, Father Anthony kneeled before the statue of Mary in the church. His rosary dangled before him, draped among his fingers, swinging gently. In the silence of the church, he heard the main door open and closed behind him, but thought nothing of it. He heard the footsteps falling on the concrete floor but, again, just assumed it was a parishioner coming to pray. That's when a familiar voice broke the silence.

"Father Anthony?"

The young priest whirled around.

"Jared...." Father Anthony stood up and walked to the teenage boy, smiling, arms outstretched.

Jared hugged him tightly.

"How are you, Jared? How are things at home? Come....let's go sit down...." They walked over to an empty pew together.

"Things are good, Father. Things are really good."

Father Anthony beamed with joy. "Wow - I did not expect you to say that.....But that's great!"

"Yeah....it's a bit of a miracle."

"Well - what's been going on? Did your father press charges?"

“No, Father....he didn’t. He and I talked after he was released from the hospital. He was in there for about a week....I banged him up pretty good.....broke his nose....busted a couple ribs....” Jared’s eyes welled up with tears. “But, even after all that, he understands why I did what I did. He finally understands.”

Father Anthony nodded, his own eyes beginning to water. “That’s amazing, Jared...Good for you!”

Jared nodded. “Yeah. But that’s not even the best part!”

“And that is?”, Father Anthony asked, his curiosity peaked.

Jared beamed with happiness. “He’s quit drinking. He stopped....just like that.....cold turkey. He’s a new man, Father....Just this morning he woke me up early and wanted me to go out with him to play some catch like we used to....It was below freezing out and snowing and we probably looked like idiots but there we were....like the old days....like we used to be."

Father Anthony was speechless. All he could do was smile and nod.

"Thank you, Father....you've helped my family so much...."

Father Anthony shook his head. "Thank Him..." He pointed to the giant crucifix that hung above the altar. "I had nothing to do with this."

They sat there, facing each other, talking for what seemed like forever, until they both realized how late it was getting.

Climbing to their feet, they walked to the door together. Reaching the end of the aisle, Jared stopped and turned to Father Anthony, smiling. “Thanks again, Father. It was great getting to know you.”

Father Anthony squeezed his arm. “My pleasure.”

Pushing open the heavy oak doors, Jared looked back once more and waved.

Mackenzie was brought back to the present by a hand gently touching her shoulder. It was the man next to her, gently urging her forward for Communion. She smiled and thanked him and filed out of the pew and into the Communion line that was slowly making its way to the front of the church.

That fateful night at her house was the last time she got to see Father Anthony. Two months after her father was released from the hospital, newly sober, he was offered a foreman position in an auto plant out of state, which he accepted. They packed up and moved soon after, putting the house up for sale. The rest of her years growing up were happy ones. Laughter and joy filled their new home. He had become the daddy that she had wanted all her life.

Her entire life she had cherished those memories of time spent with Father Anthony learning about her faith. He had been her safe haven in the midst of a storm. He had been her family's saving grace. She remembered a time spent wondering if she learned how to pray, then maybe God would stop her daddy from drinking.

Mackenzie looked up at the crucifix above the altar. It was the same one that hung there when she was a little girl. Smiling, she thanked God for answering her prayers. It seems he had heard them after all.

AFTERWORD

I would like to take this opportunity to thank some people, who, without their support, this book would never have been possible. First and foremost, my mother, Peggy Shather, who instilled in me such a tremendous love of books at such an early age. Thank you, mom, for sharing with me your love of reading. Second, my husband, Robert Okalski, for believing in me and putting up with my cluttered bookshelves and endless notebooks that I refuse to get rid of or throw away. Third, my wonderful friends, here in Houston, as well as back home in Detroit, who inspire me to no end and who keep pushing me to "get my stuff out there" - I love you all. And last but definitely not least, my best friend, Anne Springstead (springsteadanne@yahoo.com) who is not only a wonderful and caring person, but who is an amazingly talented artist - Thank you for designing my book cover - You do awesome work!!